mark Houde

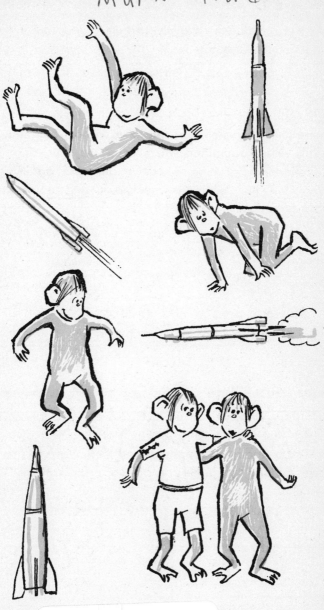

WHY THIS IS AN EASY READER

- This story has been carefully written to keep the young reader's interest high.

- It is told in a simple, open style, with a strong rhythm that adds enjoyment both to reading aloud and silent reading.

- There is a very high percentage of words repeated. It is this skillful repetition which helps the child to read independently. Seeing words again and again, he "practices" the vocabulary he knows, and learns with ease the words that are new.

- Only 156 different words have been used, with plurals and root words counted once.

  79 words—half the total vocabulary—are used at least three times.

  23 words are used at least 10 times.

  Some words have been used 48 times.

ABOUT THIS STORY

- This story is based on an actual event—the launching of our first monkey into space. It is a subject of high interest to today's youngsters, and lends itself to dramatization and the discussion of space exploration.

The Monkey in the Rocket

Story by
JEAN BETHELL
Pictures by
SERGIO LEONE
Editorial Consultant:
LILIAN MOORE

WONDER BOOKS
A Division of Grosset & Dunlap, Inc.
New York, N.Y. 10010

Introduction

These books are meant to help the young reader discover what a delightful experience reading can be. The stories are such fun that they urge the child to try his new reading skills. They are so easy to read that they will encourage and strengthen him as a reader.

The adult will notice that the sentences aren't too long, the words aren't too hard, and the skillful repetition is like a helping hand. What the child will feel is: "This is a good story—and I can read it myself!"

For some children, the best way to meet these stories may be to hear them read aloud at first. Others, who are better prepared to read on their own, may need a little help in the beginning—help that is best given freely. Youngsters who have more experience in reading alone—whether in first or second or third grade—will have the immediate joy of reading "all by myself."

These books have been planned to help all young readers grow—in their pleasure in books and in their power to read them.

Lilian Moore
Specialist in Reading
Formerly of Division of Instructional Research,
New York City Board of Education

Sam and Bam are monkeys.

They are very special monkeys.

And they live in

a very special place.

Some monkeys live in the trees.

They swing and swing

from tree to tree.

Some monkeys live in the zoo.

They jump and jump

from swing to swing.

But Sam and Bam are
very special monkeys.
They live at the
Blue Sky Rocket Base.

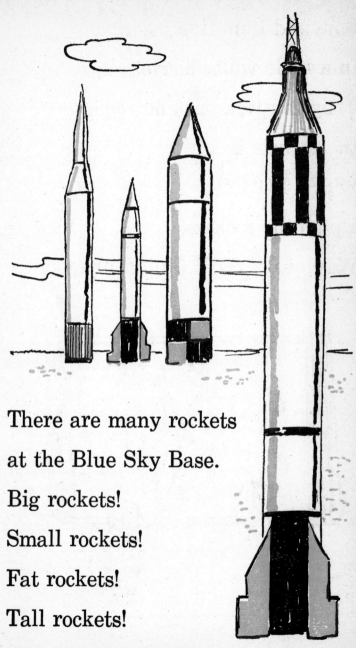

There are many rockets
at the Blue Sky Base.
Big rockets!
Small rockets!
Fat rockets!
Tall rockets!

13

Sam and Bam live

in a little white house.

They can look out and see

the rockets go up.

SSSSS-BOOM!

Up go the rockets!

Way, way, WAY up into the sky!

The biggest one of all

is Rocket 6.

It is a very special rocket.

When Rocket 6 goes up,

there will be a monkey in it!

The very first monkey

to go up in a rocket!

Will it be Sam?

Or will it be Bam?

Captain Jim wants to know.

He is the one who will

send the rocket up.

Doctor Bob wants to know.
He is the one who
takes care of the monkeys.

"Which monkey will go?"

asks Captain Jim.

"Let's find out now,"

says Doctor Bob.

Doctor Bob puts Sam and Bam

into a special chair.

The chair goes flip-flop.

Over and over!

Round and round they go!

Faster and faster and faster!

Then they stop.

Bam gets out of the chair.

Poor Bam!

Sam gets out of the chair.

Captain Jim laughs.

"Look at Sam!" he says.

"He likes to go round and round."

"Now let's try this,"
says Doctor Bob.
He puts Sam and Bam
into a special swing.

Up goes the swing.

Way, way up high.

24

Then down they come.

Down, down, down!

Faster and faster!

Just in time a parachute opens!

Just in time Sam and Bam

stop falling!

Slowly, slowly, they come down.

Bam gets out of the swing.

Poor Bam!

Sam gets out of the swing.

Captain Jim laughs again.

"Look at Sam!" he says.

"He likes to come down

in a parachute."

"We must do one more thing,"

says Doctor Bob.

This is what he does to Bam.

This is what he hears:

Bing-bang! Boom-boom!

"Poor Bam!" says Doctor Bob.

"You do not have to go up

in the rocket."

This is what he does to Sam.

This is what he hears:

"Bump-bump, bump-bump,

bump-bump."

"Sam is fine," says Doctor Bob.

"He is the one who will go.

Sam will be the first monkey

to ride in a rocket!"

Now the big day is here.

Rocket 6 will go up today!

Sam gets into his rocket suit.

He likes the way he looks.

"Now, Sam," says Doctor Bob,

"get into your special chair."

Sam gets in and sits back.

He likes his special chair.

"Good luck, Sam!" says Doctor Bob.

Then he shuts the door.

Doctor Bob and the men

take Sam away.

They take him up

to the top of Rocket 6.

They put Sam inside the rocket.

"Good-by, Sam," says Doctor Bob.

"Good-by, Sam," say the men.

Then they all go away,

and Sam is all alone.

"Now for the countdown,"
says Captain Jim.

"Ten,

Nine,

Eight,

Seven,

Six,

Five,

Four,

Three,

Two,

One. . . . .

FIRE!!!"

BOOM!

Out comes red fire!

WHOOSH!

Out comes white smoke!

Up goes the rocket!

UP! UP! UP!

Way up into the sky

UP! UP! UP!

Faster and faster it goes.

UP! UP! UP!

till no one can see it!

Doctor Bob looks up at the sky.

Will he ever see Sam again?

Will Sam come down?
If he does, he will come down
way out on the water.
A big boat
takes the men there.

The men look up at the sky.

Where is Sam?

Doctor Bob thinks,

Will I ever see Sam again?

Then they see something,

way, way up in the sky.

Something is falling!

Down, down, down!

What is it?

It is Sam!

He is falling!

"Will he be all right?"

ask the men.

"I hope so!"

says Doctor Bob.

Down, down comes Sam.

Faster and faster!

Just in time a parachute opens!

Just in time Sam stops falling!

Then he comes down slowly.

"He did not come down
in the right place,"
says Doctor Bob.
"But he *did* come down.
Now we must get him
out of the water."

The big boat takes the men
to Sam.

The men take Sam out of the water.

Is he all right?

Doctor Bob cannot wait
to find out.
He is the one
to open the door.

OUT POPS SAM!

"Hooray for Sam!" say the men.

"Hooray! Hooray! Hooray!"

"You did it, Sam!" says Doctor Bob.

"You rode a rocket into the sky!"

"How does he feel?" ask the men.

"We will see," says Doctor Bob.

This is what he does.

And this is what *Sam* does!

Sam feels fine!

Sam says something
to Doctor Bob.
"What did he say?"
ask the men.

Doctor Bob laughs.

"Sam says he likes

to ride in rockets.

And next time

he's going to the moon!"

CHOOSE FROM THESE EASY READERS

5901 Will You Come to My Party?
5902 Hurry Up, Slowpoke
5903 Mr. Pine's Mixed-up Signs
5904 The Adventures of Silly Billy
5905 The Secret Cat
5906 Billy Brown Makes Something Grand
5907 Miss Polly's Animal School
5908 The Duck on the Truck
5909 A Train for Tommy
5910 Surprise in the Tree
5911 The Monkey in the Rocket
5912 Billy Brown: The Baby Sitter
5913 Fly-Away at the Air Show
5914 Arty the Smarty
5915 The Surprising Pets of Billy Brown
5916 Barney Beagle
5917 I Made a Line
5918 Laurie and the Yellow Curtains
5919 Grandpa's Wonderful Glass
5920 Benjamin in the Woods
5921 Barney Beagle Plays Baseball
5922 The Day Joe Went to the Supermarket
5923 Question and Answer Book
5924 Jokes and Riddles
5925 Let Papa Sleep!
5926 The Surprise in the Story Book
5927 The Big Green Thing
5928 The Boy Who Fooled the Giant
5929 More Jokes and Riddles
5930 Too Many Pockets
5931 The Clumsy Cowboy
5932 Cat in the Box
5933 How the Animals Get to the Zoo
5934 The Birthday Party
5935 Little Gray Mouse and the Train

61

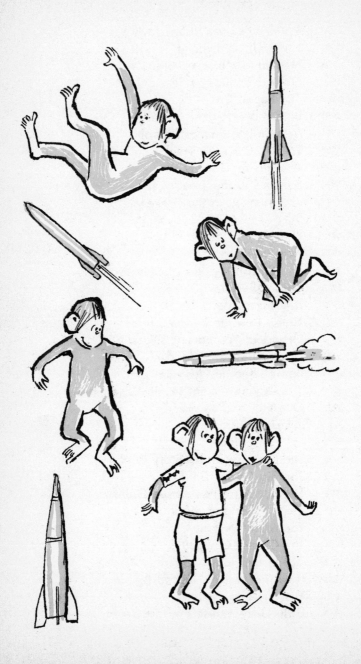